PEDRO

PEDRO THE NINJA

WITHDRAWN

by Fran Manushkin

illustrated by
Tammie Lyon

PICTURE WINDOW BOOKS
a capstone imprint

Pedro is published by Picture Window Books,
a Capstone Imprint
1710 Roe Crest Drive
North Mankato, Minnesota 56003
www.mycapstone.com

Text © 2018 Fran Manushkin
Illustrations © 2018 Picture Window Books

Library of Congress Cataloging-in-Publication Data is available on the Library of Congress website.

ISBN: 978-1-5158-1904-2 (library binding)
ISBN: 978-1-5158-1906-6 (paperback)
ISBN: 978-1-5158-1908-0 (eBook PDF)

Summary: After watching a ninja cartoon, Pedro dreams of being a ninja himself. Luckily, his dad gets him karate lessons. With hardwork and a little practice, maybe Pedro can become ninja star, just like the ones he sees in the movies!

Designer: Tracy McCabe
Design Elements: Shutterstock

Printed and bound in the USA.
010370F17

Table of Contents

Chapter 1

Karate Class

Pedro and Paco were

watching a ninja cartoon.

"Wow!" said Paco. "That

kick was awesome."

"I want to be in a ninja

movie," said Pedro.

He yelled, "Hi-YA!"

Oops! Pedro kicked a chair.

"Ouch!" he said. "Being a

ninja is tricky."

"I can help you," said

Pedro's dad. "Would you like

to take karate lessons?"

"For sure!" said Pedro.

His dad got Pedro a robe called a *gi.* "Wow!" Pedro said. "I look cool!"

"You do!" said Paco. "I wish I could go to class."

"Maybe next year," said his dad.

JoJo and Katie were in

Pedro's class. Everyone bowed

to the teacher, Sensei Kono.

He said, "The first thing

you will learn is this stance."

Pedro did the stance over
and over.

He told JoJo, "I feel like
a statue."

"But you look fierce,"
said Katie.

At the next class, Sensei Kono showed them the side kick. It was tricky. It took balance and lots of practice.

Pedro loved side kicking!

He showed Paco how to do it.

Peppy tried it too. He

kicked over his food bowl.

Every day after

school, Pedro and his

friends pretended they

were in a ninja movie.

"Let's practice our kicks,"
said JoJo.

Oops! She kicked a tree
and apples began falling —
toward Paco's head!

"Hi-YA!" yelled Pedro,

blocking the apples.

"Cool moves!" said Katie.

"I'm almost a ninja star,"

said Pedro. "It won't be long!"

Punches were the most fun.

Pedro punched beach balls

and balloons.

Pop! Pop! Pop!

No more balloons.

Pedro told Paco, "Ninja
stars are always sneaky."

Pedro practiced being
sneaky by trying to grab
cookies before supper.

"Hi-YA!" yelled his mom.

"Caught you!"

She was sneaky too.

Chapter 3
Ninja Stars

Pedro and Paco played ninja

in their room.

"Hi-YA!" Pedro yelled,

jumping out of the closet.

Paco screamed and laughed.

"You know," Pedro told

Paco, "we are having so much

fun, it's okay if we aren't

ninja movie stars."

"Is that so?" said their dad.

The next day, Pedro's friends came over to see a new ninja movie.

"This is a great one," said Pedro's mom.

"I'll say!" His dad winked.

Surprise! The ninjas were
Pedro and his friends!

Pedro's dad was sneaky.
While they were doing karate,
he was making action videos.

"We didn't look too fierce
at the start," said Pedro.

"Right!" said Katie. "But we
got better and better."

"We are the coolest,"

said Pedro.

"We are ninja stars,"

said JoJo.

"Hi-YA!" they yelled.

And they all took a bow.

About the Author

Fran Manushkin is the author of many popular picture books, including *Happy in Our Skin*; *Baby, Come Out!*; *Latkes and Applesauce: A Hanukkah Story*; *The Tushy Book*; *Big Girl Panties*; and *Big Boy Underpants*. Fran writes on her beloved Mac computer in New York City, without the help of her two naughty cats, Chaim and Goldy.

About the Illustrator

Tammie Lyon began her love for drawing at a young age while sitting at the kitchen table with her dad. She continued her love of art and eventually attended the Columbus College of Art and Design, where she earned a bachelor's degree in fine art. After a brief career as a professional ballet dancer, she decided to devote herself full-time to illustration. Today she lives with her husband, Lee, in Cincinnati, Ohio. Her dogs, Gus and Dudley, keep her company as she works in her studio.

Glossary

awesome (AW-suhm)—extremely good

balance (BA-luhnts)—to keep steady and not fall over

fierce (FEERS)—daring and dangerous

gi (GHEE)—a judo, karate, or tae kwon do uniform

karate (ka-RAH-tee)—a martial art using controlled kicks and punches

ninja (NIN-juh)—someone who is highly trained in Japanese martial arts and stealth; ninjas were often used as spies.

sensei (SEN-say)—a teacher or instructor of martial arts, such as karate

sneaky (SNEEK-ee)—able to move in a secret manner

stance (STANS)—the position of a fighter's feet and body

Let's Talk

1. The ninja cartoon inspired Pedro to take karate. What do you think he liked about the cartoon? Has a TV show or book ever inspired you to learn something new? Talk about it!

2. Do you think that Pedro is a good big brother to Paco? Why or why not?

3. At the end, Pedro says that the kids were not fierce ninjas at first, but Katie points out that they got better and better. Explain what they did to get better at karate.

Let's Write

1. Ninjas are described as fierce in this story. What else might be described as fierce? Make a list of five or more ideas.

2. Imagine that Pedro really was a ninja star. What would his movie be called? What would it be about?

3. Write down three facts about karate or ninjas. If you can't think of three, ask a grown-up to help you find some in a book or on the computer.

JOKE AROUND

★ How did the ninja beat the pig?
with a pork chop

★ What do ninjas say when they
see you?
"Hi-YA!"

★ What do ninjas drink
during the summer?
kara-TEA

★ Why was the ninja kicked out
of Hollywood?
for throwing stars

★ What is the ninja's favorite seafood?
swordfish

★ What was the ninja told after a job interview?
"You're hiya-d!"

★ What football position do ninjas like most?
kicker

THE FUN DOESN'T STOP HERE!

Discover more at www.capstonekids.com

- ★ Videos & Contests
- ★ Games & Puzzles
- ★ Friends & Favorites
- ★ Authors & Illustrators

Find cool websites and more books like this one at www.facthound.com. Just type in the Book ID: 9781515819042 and you're ready to go!